lauren child

some things are just a bit more special

But excuse me THAT is My book

dial books for young readers

Charlie and Lola ™

Text based on script written by Bridget Hurst and Carol Noble

Illustrations from the TV animation produced by Tiger Aspect

DIAL BOOKS FOR YOUNG READERS
A division of Penguin Young Readers Group
Published by The Penguin Group
Penguin Group (USA) Inc., 375 Hudson Street, New York, NY 10014, U.S.A.
Penguin Group (Canada), 90 Eglinton Avenue East, Suite 700, Toronto, Ontario, Canada M4P 2Y3
(a division of Pearson Penguin Canada Inc.)
Penguin Books Ltd, 80 Strand, London WC2R ORL, England • Penguin Ireland, 25 St. Stephen's Green, Dublin 2, Ireland (a division of Penguin Books Ltd.)
Penguin Books India Pvt Ltd, 11 Community Centre, Panchsheel Park, New Delhi - 110 017, India. • Penguin Group (NZ), Cnr Airborne and Rosedale Roads, Albany, Auckland, New Zealand
(a division of Pearson New Zealand Ltd). • Penguin Books (South Africa) (Pty) Ltd, 24 Sturdee Avenue, Rosebank, Johannesburg 2196, South Africa.
Penguin Books Ltd, Registered Offices: 80 Strand, London WC2R ORL, England.www.penguin.com
First published by Puffin Books 2005

Text based on script written by Bridget Hurst and Carol Noble.
Summary: When Lola's favorite book is not on the library's shelf,
her older brother, Charlie, tries to find another book she will enjoy.
ISBN 0-8037-3096-9

I have this little sister, Lola.
     She is small and very funny.
Lola loves reading and she really loves books.
     But at the moment there is
one book that is extra specially special.

One day, Lola says,
    "Charlie, Dad says he will take
us to the library and we must go
    right now and get
        Beetles, Bugs, and Butterflies."

Lola loves Beetles, Bugs, and Butterflies.

I say,
    "But Dad took that book out
                for you last time . . .
And the time before that . . ."

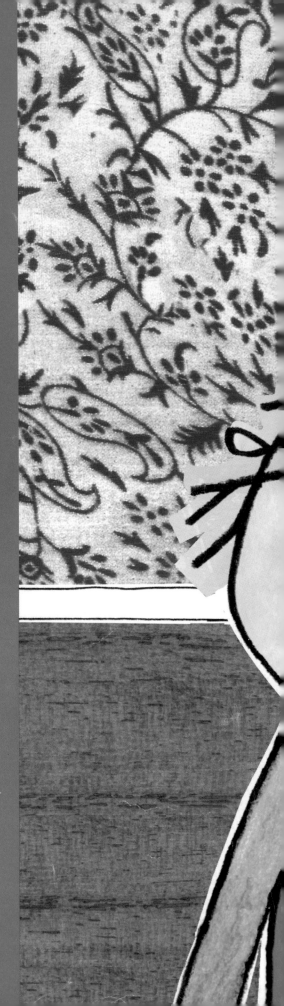

Then Lola says,
    "But Charlie, Beetles, Bugs, and Butterflies is a very special book that is my favorite and I really need it.

Now.

    Now.

        Now.

            Now.

                Now!

Don't you know Beetles, Bugs, and Butterflies is the best book in the whole world?"

And Lola says,

"You see, Charlie,

the b^ugs are quite bu^{gg}y

and the butterflies are really beautiful and

the beetles are...

very silly."

The beetle gets stuck!
And his legs are very funny!

And he

can't

turn

over!

I say,
"I know that, Lola.
Come on.
Dad's waiting."

"All his funny
little legs. Charlie!"

When we get to the library,
Lola is still saying,
      "Beetles, Bugs, and Butterflies
is the very best book in the world
         because you learn a lot and
it is very great and extremely very
interesting.
And . . .
      And I really, really
               must get it."

When we get inside
I have to say,

"Shh! Lola, it's a library.
We have to be quiet."

Lola says,
"But I can't find
my book, Charlie."

And I say,
"Then why don't you
try looking for it

in all the books
beginning with B?"

So Lola says,

"B, B, B . . . Where is my book?
Where can it be?"

I say, "Lola! Be quiet!"

She says,

"I am being quiet, Charlie!"

I say, "Shhhhh!"

She says, "I am shushing!
It's not there!
My book's not there!"

I say, "Lola! Be quiet!"
Lola says, "But Charlie, **My book** is lost!
It is completely not there!"

I say,
"Lola, remember this is a library,
so someone must have borrowed it."

Lola says,
"But Beetles, Bugs,
and Butterflies
is **My book**."

I say,
"But it's not **your** library.
Someone else obviously
wanted to **read** your book."

Lola says,
"But they can't. It's **My book**."

So I say, "Lola, just think.
There are hundreds and hundreds of other books
in the library to choose from.

There are spy books and dinosaur books. Adventure books

and scary books.

Books about princes,
airplanes, and astronauts.

Books about castles,
dragons, and volcanoes,

monsters,

mountains, and pixies.   And books about Romans."

فورج

România

I say,
"Look! Romans! This one tells you
all about history in the Roman times.
Like how the Romans built long, straight roads
and rode chariots and had
fights with swords."

oma`li

rumi

римский

ro-man

római

But Lola says,
"Too many **big** words, Charlie.

римски

로마

Rómv

Römer

zymski

România

latinluk

So I say,
"Okay Lola, let's try to find
a book with more pictures and less words.

How about this? An encyclopedia.
It's got millions of drawings and millions of facts.
You can learn about everything.
Look, this page is all about helicopters."

I say,
"You might be right, Lola,
          but see what you
    think of this . . .
        It's a pop-up book."

But Lola says,

"A book that has

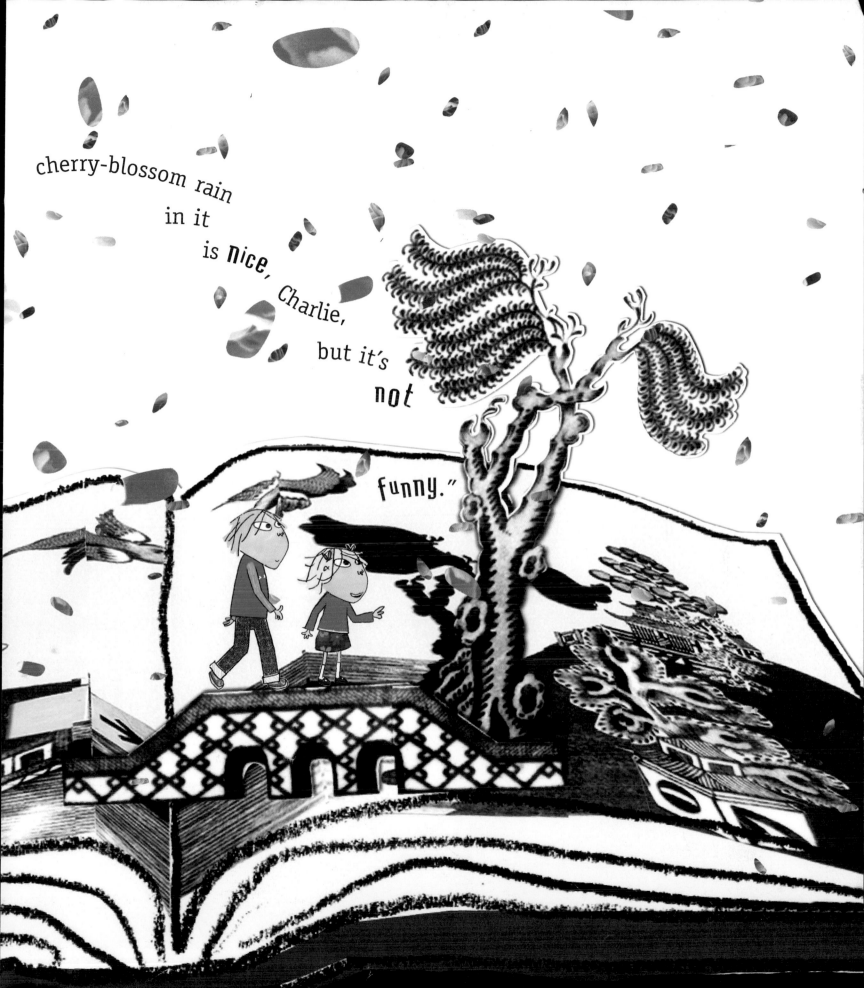

Then Lola says,
"Beetles, Bugs, and Butterflies
is really funny
and makes me

laugh

and

laugh

and

laugh..."

I say,

"So it's an **animal** book you want.

        A book with . . . lots of pictures . . . a story . . .
no **big** words . . . and animals that make you laugh."

        Lola says, "Yep."

I say, "How about this, Lola?! Cheetahs and Chimpanzees."

        Lola says, "Are there
beetles, bugs, and butterflies in it?!"

        I say, "No, there are
cheetahs and chimpanzees.
Give it a try, Lola. Please."

Lola says, "Okay Charlie,
        I will. But it won't
be as good as . . .

"Beetles, Bugs, and Butterflies!

Oh no, Charlie! Look! That girl's got My book! I don't think she knows it is My book!

"No, noO...

Just wait...

That's **my**...

That's **my**...

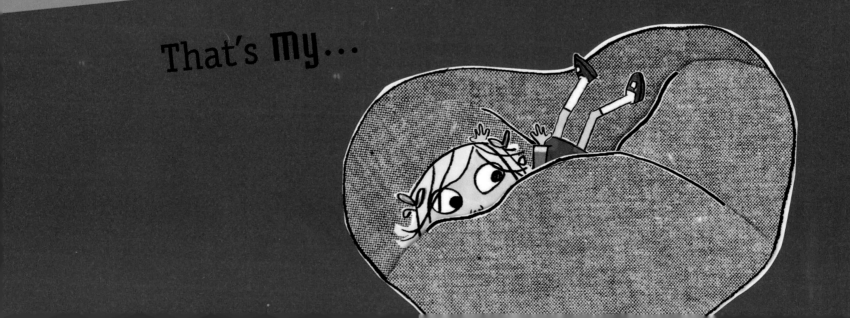

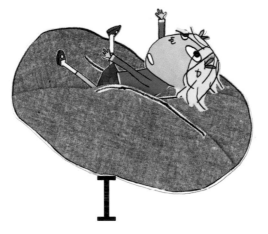

I

just

like

My book,

Charlie!"

Lola says,
"I want **my book**, Charlie!"
And I say,
    "But you said you would try
            Cheetahs and Chimpanzees."

    Lola says,
"Well . . . I'll try it,
        but it won't be as good
    as Beetles, Bugs, and Butterflies."

But then Lola says,
"Oh! Look at that. The **cheetahs** are very **fast** and the **chimpanzees**

are very cheeky and in fact, you know what, Charlie . . . ?

"This book is probably
the most best book in the whole wide world
because it is so interesting and so lovely
and you know it has the absolutely best pictures of any book ever
and the baby chimps are very funny . . ."